Gabriel's Horn

For Carolina Martinez
–E. A. K.

To my grandmother
–M. S.

KAR-BEN PUBLISHING, INC.
A division of Lerner Publishing Group, Inc.
241 First Avenue North
Minneapolis, MN 55401 USA
1-800-4-KARBEN
Website address: www.karben.com

Library of Congress Cataloging-in-Publication Data

Names: Kimmel, Eric A., author. | Surducan, Maria, illustrator.
Title: Gabriel's horn / by Eric A. Kimmel ; illustrated by Maria Surducan.
Description: Minneapolis, MN : Kar-Ben Publishing, a division of Lerner Publishing Group, [2016] | 2016
Identifiers: LCCN 2015040980 (print) | LCCN 2015041362 (ebook) |
    ISBN 9781467789363
    (lb : alk. paper) | ISBN 9781467794176 (pb) | ISBN 9781512409383 (eb pdf)
Subjects: | CYAC: Fortune—Fiction.
Classification: LCC PZ7.K5648 Ga 2016 (print) | LCC PZ7.K5648 (ebook) | DDC
    [E]—dc23
LC record available at http://lccn.loc.gov/2015040980

Manufactured in the United States of America
1 – CG – 7/15/16

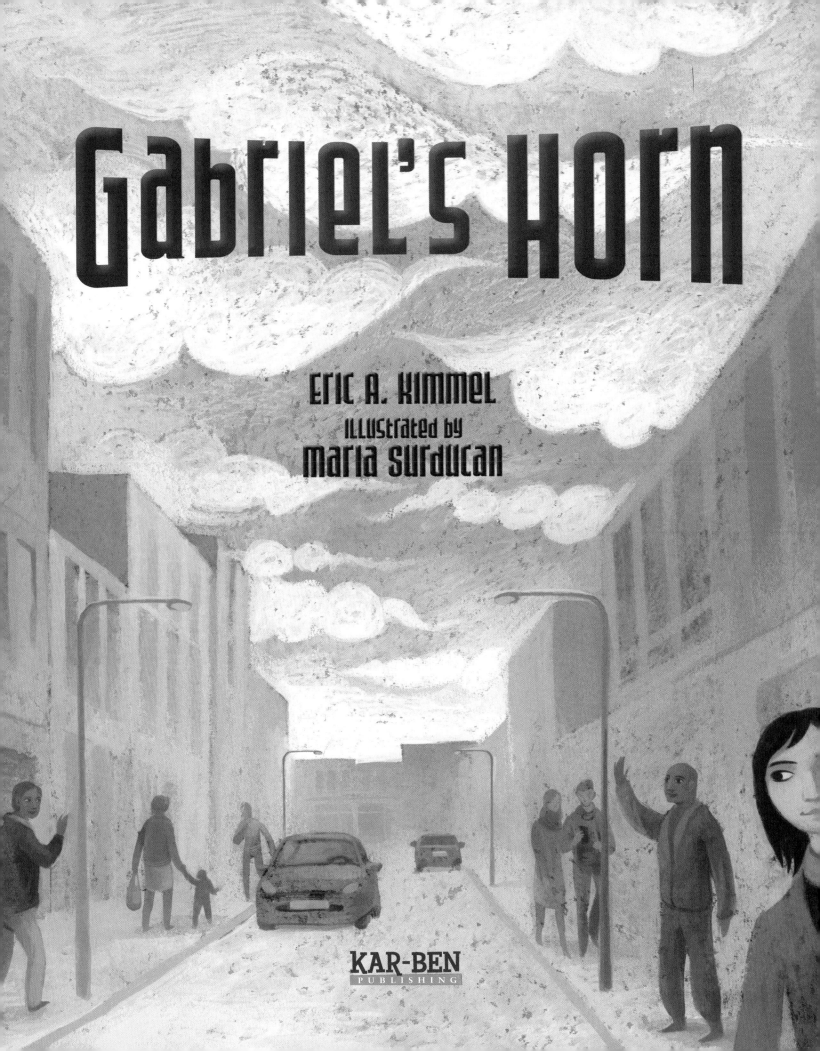

Gabriel's Horn

Eric A. Kimmel

Illustrated by
Maria Surducan

KAR-BEN
PUBLISHING

Friday had come, the end of the week. Gabriel hurried home from school to help Mom prepare for Shabbat. This was no ordinary Shabbat. It was Erev Rosh Hashanah, the beginning of the *Yamim Nora'im*, the days from Rosh Hashanah to Yom Kippur—the holiest days of the year.

Gabriel helped Mom prepare the special round challah for the holiday. He hoped the new year would be a good one, but he had his doubts.

Mom and Dad's little antique store was barely surviving. So many other businesses in their neighborhood—the ice cream store, the bookshop, the craft store, the pizza restaurant—were gone. Gabriel's parents looked worried most of the time.

"Maybe next year will be better," Gabriel said.

"From your mouth to God's ear," Mom replied. That was her way of saying, "May your wish come true." Gabriel was about to say, "Amen," when someone knocked on the door.

Gabriel ran to the door, expecting one of their neighbors. Instead, it was someone he had never seen before—a soldier. The soldier held a battered leather case in both hands.

"Are you the folks who own the antique store?"

"That's us," Gabriel said as Mom joined him at the door.

"I'm hoping you can help me," the soldier said. "I'm going overseas. I don't know when I'll be back, and I can't take my horn with me."

The soldier held up the case. "It belonged to my grandpa, Big Daddy. He was a musician. I don't play. Never had a lick of talent. But this horn is precious to me. I want to leave it with people who will take care of it while I'm gone. Can you do that for me?"

"I don't know," Mom said. "We sell antiques. We don't store them . . ."

"Please, Mom," said Gabriel. "It won't take up much room. We can keep it in the closet." There was something unusual about this soldier. Gabriel could feel it. He knew this request was important.

"Thank you. You won't be sorry. Big Daddy always said that horn brings good luck." The soldier handed the case to Gabriel. Then he turned and started toward the stairs.

Mom called after him, "Wait! How can we contact you?"

The soldier answered, "I'll contact you."

"Gabriel! Run after him!"

Gabriel put down the case. He ran down the stairs, hoping to catch the soldier.

But the man had vanished.

Gabriel ran outside. He looked up and down the street. "Did you see where that soldier went?" he asked two boys who were sitting on the curb.

"What soldier?" they asked.

Back in the apartment, Mom opened the case to have a look at the mysterious horn. The brass was dark with tarnish. A spiderweb covered the bell.

"This horn looks as if no one's played it in years!" Mom exclaimed. "You'd think he'd take better care of it if it was so important to him."

"It might look better if we clean it," Gabriel suggested.

Mom rinsed out a rag to wipe off the dust and cobwebs. But when she tried to polish the horn, she couldn't make it any shinier. Not even the special polish she used for the Shabbat candlesticks worked. The horn remained dark with tarnish.

Mom sighed and put the horn back in its case. "Well, we've done our best." She went back to the kitchen. Just then, Gabriel heard another knock at the door. He ran to open it. Maybe the soldier had come back.

Instead, two girls greeted him.

"Hi! We're collecting money for a clothing drive at our school. We're going to buy winter coats for kids whose families can't afford them."

"That's a great idea." Gabriel gave the girls some change—the last of his allowance. "I wish I had more."

"Every bit helps," one girl said. "Thank you!"

Gabriel went back into the living room. Mom had left the horn's case open. The horn was still tarnished, but now he could see a streak of polished brass shining on its bell.

Over the next week, Gabriel noticed more changes. He won first prize in his school's book drive by reading the most pages and collecting the most pledge money to buy books for the library. And another polished spot appeared on the horn.

A few days later, Dad came home with amazing news.

"This morning I found a rolled-up painting in the alley. I could tell it was something special, so I asked around. It turns out that the painting was stolen from a museum. It has to go back to the museum. But we get a reward for finding it!"

"A reward?" echoed Gabriel, remembering the soldier's words about good fortune.

His father nodded. "It won't make us rich, but we won't have to worry about money for a while."

"And we can do more things to help the people in our neighborhood," said Gabriel. "Isn't that what good fortune is for?"

As time passed, Gabriel's family helped
build a new playground at the park.

They bought furniture for a family who
had just moved to America.

They donated food to the neighborhood food shelf.

Meanwhile the antique store did better than ever before, until it became known as one of the finest in the city. It seemed the more Gabriel's family helped others, the more prosperous they became.

Seven years went by. Gabriel was in high school. He had just come home one afternoon when he heard a knock at the door.

There stood the soldier. He looked exactly the same.

"Remember me?" he said. "I've come for my horn."

"I knew you'd be back," Gabriel said. He went to get the horn from the closet.

As he handed back the case, Gabriel said, "You're not really a soldier, are you? I think I know who you are."

The soldier didn't answer.

"I always suspected that our good luck came with your horn," Gabriel added. "And now it's time to give the horn—and the luck—back."

"That's how it goes," the soldier said.

He opened the battered case. A flash of gleaming brass lit up the room. There wasn't a speck of tarnish left.

"I don't know how that happened," said Gabriel. "We gave up trying to polish it long ago."

"Yet every time you did something for someone else, it grew a little brighter," said the soldier. He closed the case and handed it back to Gabriel.

"Do you know how old this horn is? It's older than the world. In all the time this horn has existed, no one ever used its blessing better than your family. That old horn never shined brighter than it does now. You've earned the right to keep it."

"What will we do with it?" Gabriel asked, looking down at the battered case. "Nobody in our family can play it."

When he looked up, the soldier was gone.

Every year at Rosh Hashanah,
Gabriel told the story of the horn
to his children and grandchildren.
When he finished, he would open
the case and show them the horn.

Those who have seen it
say that it shines brighter
than a thousand suns.

Author's Note

Tzedekah—helping those in need—is one of the cornerstones of Judaism. While the Hebrew word *tzedakah* is often translated as "charity," it really means "righteousness." Since the days of the prophets, showing compassion for the poor and the less fortunate has always been important.

Children learn to value tzedakah through the example of their parents and other adults in their lives. Collecting money for charitable causes, donating unneeded toys and clothes, and volunteering at a food bank or homeless shelter are only a few of the ways of making tzedakah a family tradition.

This story is a modernized version of one I wrote several years ago for a collection of Rosh Hashanah stories called *Days of Awe.* The original story was called "The Samovar." It was based on a famous story by the great Yiddish writer I. L. Peretz called "Seven Years," which in turn is based on one of the many legends about Eliyahu ha'Navi— Elijah the Prophet.

According to the Talmud, Elijah sometimes returns to help people in need and to encourage others to do so by example.

Elijah assumes different disguises when he returns. He could be the man sitting next to you on the bus, the boy on the skateboard, the beggar standing in the street, or the nurse taking your temperature.

Or the soldier standing at your door.

—Eric A. Kimmel